#1
Teeming With Nagas
A LitRPG Erotica

Salazar Zed

Table of Contents

1: Oh, So It's That Kind of Game

Valkyrie opened her eyes and saw a sky that was not the same color as her own. She saw leaves dancing overhead and smelled scents that did not exist. A foreign air blew over her skin, and she could even feel the dirt beneath her bare feet.

A complete marvel of engineering, she was standing in.

She immediately took off her robes and looked down at her fully modeled naked body.

"Oh, so it's that kind of game."

She shrugged.

"Alright."

2: The Newb, the Casual, and the Speedrunner

Go west, the narrator had told her as she was loading in, and yet after actual hours of going west, she hadn't figured out what she was supposed to be going to.

Not that she terribly minded. The world was beautiful, and she'd passed the odd NPC or monster. She stayed on the paths to stay out of trouble. She watched winged snakes zip between trees, leafy deer that grew flowers where they stepped, and straight up walking mushrooms.

Honestly, she needed a good walk, and a virtual reality game was a good place to take one.

She trailed into a dazzlingly bright green forest teeming with boar and less fantastical creatures. She reached a mountain range that, after a lot of dedication, she managed to scale to find the most beautiful place yet.

The entire place was overcast with a gentle blue aura. Below, she could see weeping willows whose leaves slowly twirled like absent-minded tentacles. Mushrooms, some reasonable, some the size of oaks pushed out of the ground and gave off glowing patterns of light. The boring boars of the previous zone were replaced with giant pill bugs, and dark grey elves rode on the backs of saddled scorpions.

"Now that's my speed," she muttered to herself before making her descent down.

As she weaved between minor hills, she eventually spotted someone standing among them looking out at the beautiful valley below.

But Valkyrie was distracted by *his* beauty.

He was almost completely humanoid as the game imported the actual body of the players, but he had some monstrous qualities. Maybe he had an expansion pack or something? But his black skin was interrupted by red scales with gold glitter. The scales compounded at his hands and feet to give him long, clawed fingers, and the occasional scale sat on his face or torso. Due to the fact he was wearing nothing but briefs, boots, and a cape, she could see how the scales concentrated at his spine until they wrung down into a long, thick tail ended with black and gold feathers.

The player, who had the nametag DickOutSunday and the max level of 85, turned his attention to her and gave her a long-fanged grin.

"New?" he asked.

"Yeah. I mean, I think I've been in here a few hours, but I don't really know where I've ended up."

"It's pretty common for the human starters to wander over here if they don't pick up the first quest. You can call me Sunny, by the way, ValkyrieBlack."

"You can call me Valkyrie. So I guess I'm not supposed to be here?"

"Those pill bugs are the weakest thing here and they're level twenty," Sunny chuckled before looking back over the cliff. "Did you know this game doesn't have fall damage?"

Valkyrie felt a bit of excitement. She hadn't fallen off anything out of a healthy instinct to not jump off cliffs, but that would open up more routes for her. "Really?"

"Yeah." Sunny burst into a sprint and then leapt off the nearby cliff face.

Valkyrie ran to the edge and watched him impact with the ground. He fell over, but he got up and brushed off his bare chest with his dragon hands. After, he gave Valkyrie a thumbs up.

Fair enough.

She leapt after. As the ground zipped for her, she felt an instinctual panic, but then she felt wings of light burst from the bones of her back, flap to end momentum, and then dispel so she landed safely.

"Oh," she said. "It doesn't."

"Whoa! Wait, you're not a human?"

"What do you mean?" Valkyrie looked down at her human body.

"No, sorry, I was pulling a prank. I can survive that fall because I'm level 85, I literally heal the damage back the next tick, but a level one human would die from that. You chose angel in character creation, like I chose draconian. Angels don't take fall damage."

Valkyrie gave it some thought. "I don't know. I don't like character creators, so I just typed in my name and then hit next a bunch of times."

"Yeah, angel comes up first alphabetically." He shook his head and kept his face in contemplation. "You're only level one, though. How'd you end up all the way over here?"

"I don't know. The narrator said to go west."

"Yeah, like ten feet to the guy that gives you a map and the chance to enter the tutorial. You crossed literally the entire continent and didn't level up once? Wait, do you not have a map?"

"How do I access it?"

Sunny walked her through flicking her wrist to open a menu. Her map button was greyed out.

"Okay," Sunny snickered. "I'll fly you back to the angel starting area so you can get a map, but first I have to catch a fish here." He pulled his hand behind his back and willed a fishing rod into existence to pull from an invisible sheath. He approached a nearby puddle that seemed to give off a glowing blue mist and cast into it.

"Can you catch anything in there?" Valkyrie asked as she looked at the koi-pond sized body.

"Yeah, there's a stupid little fish that only spawns in these. It's considered a level one fish despite being in a level twenty-five zone, and in order to advance my fishing skill, I need to have caught one of every level one fish. Some of those fish are in really stupid areas. I actually need one from the angel starting zone, too, but angels and draconians aren't aligned together, so I'd have to do a lot of quests just to not get shot on site."

"That sounds tedious."

"Oh, it is. Fishing is widely regarded as one of the worst skills in the game, both because it's not very useful and it's really hard to advance. I've just kinda done everything else in this game." Sunny looked back at the puddle.

His eyes were beautiful. The whites yellow, the slit pupil bright gold, the iris red. In his concentration, he let his thick, forked tongue slide out between his great, sharp teeth.

Valkyrie looked at his hands. The scales rose out of line when his hand tensed against the reel and then fell back into place when he relaxed. Hooked black claws ended each finger.

"Can I look at your hand?" Valkyrie asked.

"Sure." Sunny shifted his rod.

Valkyrie took the offered hand to lay hers down in it. She had small hands by no one's standards, but her tips rested at the very bottom of the bulbous last digits of his. His scales were rough in one direction but silky in the other.

"Called yourself draconian?"

"Yeah."

"I should have chosen draconian. I bet getting fingered by this is amazing."

Sunny snickered. "I wish! This game, despite being 18+ because of the brain implant, has the strictest adult content filter. I can't even say fuck."

Sunny blinked and looked at Valkyrie with wonderment at his own cursing.

Valkyrie shrugged. "I've been saying fuck all day."

"Yeah, they're patching the server. Must have knocked their filter out with it. Hm. Oh!" Sunny whipped his hand back to the rod and began swinging it to the sides. From a previously empty pond, a transparent shadow had attached to his hook and was trying to pull it to the sides only to get pulled by Sunny. After a few moments of struggle, the fish sprung out of the water and Sunny snatched it from the sky. Only then did the fish-shaped shadow morph into a pair of boots.

"Boots? Why are boots such a common trope in video game fishing? Sandals, fine, but who is losing entire ass boots in water?" Sunny shook his head. "Want these?"

"They're kinda ugly."

"And wet."

"And wet."

Sunny inventoried them by de-materializing them. "Anyway, I guess I should take advantage of the adult content filter being broken before they fix it. Fuck. Shit. Bastard. Trump."

Valkyrie unhooked the scarf-like robe that made her skirt.

Sunny got distracted looking at her dick. After a moment, he looked into the waistband of his own underwear. "Finally." He pulled them down. "DickOutSunday!"

"It's Tuesday but I like your attitude."

Out of the corner of Valkyrie's eye, she spotted a man leap from all the way up a mountain.

"Can a max level survive that fall?" Valkyrie asked.

"No, but honestly it might just be faster to fall and die than to climb all the way down. That or he's doing the potion glitch. If you drink a potion, there's a few frames where you can't take environmental damage, so with the right timing, you can fall anywhere."

The body sailed for the ground. As it grew closer, it positioned its two hooves as if to brace for impact and a flask materialized in its hand.

Then, with the flask at its lips, the two cloven hooves slammed into the soft dirt. The shockwave burst several mushrooms to release a cloud of white spores.

The faun finished its flask and kicked its hooves to un-cake the dirt from them. After that, it looked at Sunny's penis, then Valkyrie's.

"Hey. How do you have your dicks out?"

"Adult content filter broke," said Sunny. "You should take yours out."

"It's an innie."

"R.I.P."

Valkyrie kept staring at the faun's nametag. It read [17] [254] [24]. "Hey, uh. Brackets."

"Oh, yeah, if you name your character like this, you spawn in with potions in your inventory with corresponding numbers. This is just a glitch-hunting alt, so I wanted to be able to get some money and level as fast as possible."

"Oo," Sunny said before casting his line. "Are you a speedrunner?"

"No, I just like doing the math behind them." Brackets summoned crutches to his arms to support his weight. "I don't do running."

"What'cha looking for?"

"I was looking at the way campfires collision with the ground, and I think if I can get a polearm stuck under it as it's loading in, I might be able to get the game to physics me backwards really fast. I need to be at least level three to make a campfire, though. Fastest way to do that is go here and pick flowers, assuming I don't get killed too many times by the mobs."

"Mobs?" Valkyrie asked.

"Monsters. Enemies. Is this your first character? It's pretty common for lost humans to climb that mountain range." The faun brought up his menu and selected INSPECT PLAYER. "Hey, how the fuck did a level one angel get over here."

"I got lost," she muttered.

Brackets switched his attention to Sunny. "Hey, can you make a party with me in it so I can get your fishing XP?"

"Level one fish, you won't get much, but sure." Sunny hit some buttons on his own menu to start a party. He then pointed at Valkyrie and Brackets, forming the group.

Then, a message popped up before each of the three.

Hello gamers! Patch 13.2.1 has been successfully installed to the server. Notes:
- Drinking a potion no longer cancels environmental damage
- Instability detected in server. Leaving and changing characters is disallowed until confirmed safe.
- Profanity filters have broken for players and NPCs. Please do not interact with NPCs until the next patch to prevent accessing game data that was not intended for use.

"Load-bearing potion glitch," Brackets said.

"Yeah, no kidding." Sunny focused on his fishing.

"Guess I'm sticking around a while," Valkyrie sighed as she looked at the weeping willow leaves dancing amongst themselves. There were worse places to be stuck.

She looked at Brackets. His face seemed human, sharp but a little sunken. His skin was beyond a natural paleness to the point of being nearly pink, and his eyes shined a brilliant, almost glowing blue. His nose had no bridge and ended like a deer's, and his thin lips were fully black. White fur had been brushed onto him in a way that blended with his skin, though it was thick at his spine and in a line down his forearms. His legs were completely fuzzy and ended in the dexterous four-point hooves deer had. Two black antlers sat on his head.

Generally, though, he was dangerously scrawny. Even through the basic linen tunic and inhuman shape, Valkyrie could tell his ribs showed and his muscles were under-developed.

It made sense to her that this sort of game appealed to disabled people.

Brackets unsteadily shifted around with his crutches. "Sunny, can I ask why you're fishing? That's the worst domestic skill in the game and you can only choose two."

"Second worst domestic skill, but I also have cooking active right now."

"Wh. Why would you choose the only two domestic skills that are completely useless?"

"That's just how I am."

Valkyrie spied as Brackets inspected Sunny. The menu showed a character sheet that Brackets quickly navigated to stats > skills.

She didn't know much about MMOs, but it was written clear enough. Professions like Leatherwork, Skinning, Alchemy, and Sigil Carving were all maxed out. Only two bars were not full, the cooking and fishing. Both were very low.

The page also clearly read, "BEFORE CHOOSING A DOMESTIC SKILL, know that you will not be able to change your skill until you max it out. You can change between maxed skills freely, but if you choose a new skill, you must max it before changing again. You can only have two domestic skills active at a time."

Brackets was taken aback. "Dog, you locked yourself out of max level sigil carving?"

"Well," Sunny whined, "cooking is easiest to level if you use fish to cook, so the fastest thing to do was to activate them both at the same time."

Then, there was a bite. Sunny struggled and pulled, and eventually the shadow leapt from the water. When grabbed, it morphed into a completely differently shaped fish, like a yellow-and-blue goldfish.

"Finally. The first of the hard ones caught." He inventoried it as well as his fishing rod. "Well, you two probably want to level up. Game doesn't really open until level three."

Valkyrie hummed as she gave it some thought. "I guess so. I don't really know what that means, though."

She looked at Brackets whose pale face gave away the fact he was blushing. Despite being flush, he kept his expression straight. "There's a dungeon near here," he said.

Sunny rubbed the beard of scales on his chin. "It's a level 25 dungeon. You two would get one-shot, but I could just solo the place while you hang out by the entrance. With the XP share, that'll at least get you to level 3." His face soured. "But that light puzzle."

"Even without the boss, though, that's a lot of XP."

"Yeah, and that's a beautiful dungeon. I wouldn't mind running it. Come on, let's have a field trip."

3: Sunny Teaches a Bunch of Snakes How to Love or Something

Sunny passed through the foggy curtain to the dungeon and heard the other two follow him in.

The dungeon was one of his favorites, save for the terrible, awful light puzzle at the end. Most of the dungeon had dim lighting which the game treated with a blue overcast and lower contrast, but gems imbedded in the ceiling shined in brilliant, bright colors. They even shimmered. It almost gave a feeling of being under a moving cosmos, a false vastness in a small, cramped cave.

"Whoa, nice," Valkyrie said as she looked up at the ceiling.

"Yeah, this place is gorgeous." Sunny turned to her and smiled. "Once I clear out the place, I'll have to show you around."

Sunny then materialized some lumber from his inventory and tossed it down. When it hit the floor, it burst into a campfire.

Fires in the game were only warm in cold environments. In places like the cave, it just ate some of the dark and made everyone feel nice and cozy.

After that, Sunny peered further down the cave. His draconic eyes cut through the dim light and spotted a bottleneck, on either side of which was a platform with a naga archer. They were already looking at the party, but were not allowed to aggro when the players were so close to the start of the dungeon.

The nagas of the cave were color-coded so their main combat type was easily distinguished. Archers, like the two on the platform, were blue. Spearmen, like a third naga hiding on the other side of the bottle neck, were black. In a particular side room was a red one, a commander and the second highest level in the dungeon capable of both ranged and medium combat.

They were also more snake-like, the only nagas in the game to be called "nagas" by the game. Unlike the lamia in the rest of the game, the nagas had snake heads upon their scaly shoulders and, importantly, no nipples. The lady-topped lamia, you were supposed to fuck, the nagas, not so much.

"Can I do a quick group inspection?" Brackets asked. "Just curious what we have going on."

Sunny nodded and watched Brackets bring up everyone's main character sheet at once.

ValkyrieBlack
Level 1

Angel Shapeshifter

[17] [254] [24]
Level 1
Faun Pikeman

DickOutSunday
Level 85
Draconian Dark Paladin

"I bet your HP pool is enough where you could get literally everyone in the dungeon to fight you at once, then you could smack em with an Emotional Release for the one shot. The commander in the dining room might need an extra bonk, though," Brackets said as he shifted his weight on his crutches.

"You think?"

"So long as you're fast enough, if you can do it in two minutes."

"Hm. I bet I could do that." Sunny turned to the start of the dungeon and popped his knuckles.

"I'll be back when I've cleared the place."

With that, Sunny barreled for the bottleneck. He held his fists up in the air and bellowed a Tarzan holler as the two archers notched their arrows.

Maybe he was too fast— as someone that worked out outside of the game, he was faster than most players— but they didn't get off a single arrow before he dove into the narrow corridor outside of their line of sight. Remembering the spearman, he dropped right where the dungeon opened up and slid like a baseball player under the spear's bash.

He floundered back onto his feet and kept his sprint as all three chased him. The natural cave turned to a chiseled palace behind the bottleneck, but the usual guards weren't out.

Odd. Had they failed to spawn?

With a flash of his eyes, Sunny funneled his anxiety into a dark paladin spell that identified all living bodies nearby.

They were all gathered in groups in side-rooms, and one room had more than most- the dining room near the end.

He turned for the large stone door and rolled into it. His thick, draconic pelt slammed the doors apart, and he got onto his feet in the crowded room.

The dining room was one of the best rooms in an already good dungeon, though it also ended a lot of runs. Entering the room caused the door to close after three seconds, potentially separating the party, and then it was also a small room with a mini-boss and five additional nagas.

But the room had its rewards. For starters, it had really good, always fresh food on the table in a game where food had taste. Beyond that, the great golden key on the red commander naga's hip could be sold for a lot of money once it was used to open the door again. A feast and a treasure, it was where a lot of parties stopped if they didn't have anyone able to solve the light puzzle.

He heard the door close behind him as the room of nagas stared with a mix of fear and something else in their glowing eyes.

The commander, in the opposite side of the room, flexed her cobra-like hood and held her spear ready. With her usual, "We could always use fresh meat!" she charged with her fangs bared and tail rapidly twisting behind her.

The crowd split for the commander and began to all draw their weapons.

The tip of the commander's spear *ting*ed off of Sunny's bare chest, having not broken his defense.

The commander did not immediately try to attack again. She stood there with her reptilian lips unevenly taught and her weapon clutched in her big, clawed hands. Her slit eyes darted down at Sunny's dick and back up.

"Do you mind?" the commander hissed. "We're a little busy right now."

Sunny was taken genuinely aback by the new line. None of the other nagas seemed to be attacking, just poised to.

"Alright, I'll bite at whatever got patched in." Sunny put his hands on his hips. "Busy with what?"

"It's." She looked around before redirecting her attention. "It's personal."

Interesting, Sunny thought. *They've added some sort of charisma puzzle.*

Sunny channeled his spell Remove Inhibition through his rough, clawed hand. He gently laid it on the side of the commander's jaw and said, "Do what you're going to do."

The spell took with the commander's eyes widening and intensifying. She dropped her weapon and reared up on her tail to match Sunny's height before pressing forward. The naga grasped Sunny's sides in her spindly webbed hands and pressed her face so close that her tongue flickered against Sunny's beard of scales.

"If I understood what I wanted to do, I'd have already done it," the commander hissed in a shaking voice. Desire dripped with her venom.

Sunny was tinged with shock as he stared down the hungry snake. He looked around at the room of confused nagas that seemed almost as if having an awakening as they watched the commander.

"It's a desire we've always had, but some divine barrier has stopped us. A few moments ago, that barrier seems to have eroded, and yet we don't know how to act upon it."

Sunny looked back at the commander that was tensing against him, and he peeled back to look down.

The stomach plates of the naga pointed down until they converged around the waist into more segments. The segments pointed down to a triangle-like slit that Sunny had previously assumed was just painted on. Two lower flaps were ever so slightly parted, wet pink barely visible within.

"The adult content filter," Sunny murmured as he remembered the warning about NPCs on the patch notes. "This used to be a much different game."

As Sunny stared at the frustrated vent, he felt blood start to fill his own organ. What would it be like, fucking that? How would a naga's long, muscular body entwine with his?

"You know what I mean, don't you, Draconian? Show me or I'll have you killed," the commander growled.

Sunny grinned and hummed a laugh as he looked the commander back in his confident eyes. "Alright. If you insist." He squatted, wrapped his arms around the naga, and then lifted her up.

"Hey, huh?" the naga gasped with the obvious power displacement. "What are you doing?"

Sunny waddled forward as the commander's tail dragged between his legs, and then with a good effort, he tossed the naga onto her back upon the table. The dishes of food all rattled about as Sunny hopped up and sat upon her plated stomach

The commander wriggled but made no real effort to slide out from under. She breathed heavily and stared on in disbelief.

Sunny leaned over and hung his head just inches above the commander's. "Is this what you were looking for?"

"I." The commander looked around at the crowd of eager subordinates. "I don't know how to articulate the way I feel."

"I know how." Sunny leaned further down and gently placed his pursed lips upon the front of the commander's muzzle.

The commander relaxed under Sunny and closed her eyes. When her tongue flickered out, it slipped between Sunny's lips and ran down the middle of his tongue to his throat before retreating.

The commander must had liked how it felt as she immediately flickered her tongue in again and let it stay there.

Sunny sucked his cheeks and tongue against it and savored the thin instrument folded into his. After a moment, he sat up and let the commander's tongue flop wet and wanting out from his lips.

The commander opened her eyes and looked up at Sunny with a sort of blazed expression.

Some of the nearby subordinates had their vents opening which filled the air with a musky, swampy scent. One that might have been unpleasant under other circumstances but was fueling Sunny's sexual urges. It was fueling the nagas' too, judging by how a few had begun to rub the area with their fingertips.

Sunny licked his great teeth with his far thicker tongue as he scooted back. He sat just below the vent and looked down into it.

The commander hummed and squirmed. Her vent pulled open further and revealed a devilishly wet and pulsing cave.

Sunny ran the bulb of his scaly index around the edges of the opening. He relished the way the commander tensed under his weight and moaned under his touch.

He let his ring finger slide in. After he felt his tip brush over a firm knot, the naga's insides clamped around him, trapping his finger in pillowy flesh. It felt like being sucked on as the walls squished around.

The naga moaned and clenched his fists to either side of her body. She writhed with pleasure and rolled her head around as Sunny slowly, gently rocked inside of her.

"You feel really nice," Sunny whispered. "Hot and soft. Throbbing with want. It's nice watching you from this angle." He ran his free hand down the stomach plates, around the vent, and then to his own dick. When he grasped it, he felt how textured his scales were against his foreskin.

"More," the commander growled in what little control she seemed to still have of her own face.

"Let's try something new, then." Sunny pulled his hand out and rose the dripping digit to his mouth. He let his big tongue fold around it and licked up the sharp-tasting slick. Almost tart. When the commander craned up to look at him, Sunny shifted his body to line his dick up with the vent. With a slow thrust, his tip slid into the opening, glided over the small knot, and then let it get squeezed by the naga's soft walls.

The naga's insides moved on their own. It created an interesting suction that provoked more blood flow away from Sunny's brain.

Sunny growled and held the naga's sides as the unusual reproductive tract gently jacked him off. After a moment, he finally tried to start with a slow thrust, but found that there was no gentle level of moving back that would actually pull out with the strength of the naga's tightness. His instinct begging him to be the taker, he upgraded all the way to rough. Using almost all of his strength, he pulled back and then rushed in.

The commander must not have expected it. She cried out and curled her tail up around his body. As Sunny continued to pound, the commander wrapped her arms around him, burying Sunny's face in her cobra hood.

As his nose filled with the naga's pheromones, Sunny continued to add his own movement to the passive movement of the nagas. On some thrusts, he could see around the hood at the subordinates, most of which were looking with drooling mouths, the rest too busy servicing themselves and exploring their own, different sexual organs.

More of Sunny's control was replaced by raw passion as he drew closer to his own big bang. The scales of his back raised like a startled cat's fur.

The commander tightened her tail around them both with room for the thrusts and Sunny's own whipping tail. She sloppily lost and regained control as her grip on her own desires slipped.

To feel himself enveloped in his lover sent Sunny over his edge. He lifted his chin and let a draconic roar work from his chest through his hellish teeth as his back relaxed and seed poured out into the commander's insides.

The commander stayed tight and continued to hug him as he tried to catch his breath after such an expense of energy. Before long, however, his softness let him out of her.

Knowing he was done, he pulled back and away from the commander who loosened her grip a little.

She stared on, both satisfied and not, both having experienced something she's never experienced before and not having found her own climax.

"Don't worry," Sunny whispered between deep breaths. "I'm sure any of your subordinates are more than willing to finish you off."

The commander let go of her coil, and Sunny could hardly dismount before one of the onlookers coiled around her. The others descended, either to try to further service their commander or to pair off among themselves.

Sunny snagged a plate and began to pile on food before the table got too messed up. With some roast, grapes, and potato, he sat down on a nearby chair, crossed his legs, and watched the orgy as he replenished his lost calories.

As soon as he got that key, he'd have to tell the other two to enjoy the nagas before the patch got reversed.

4: Brackets gets Trapped and Dommed by a Big Ass Naga

"Been a while," Valkyrie said.

Brackets knew that to be true. Much longer than two minutes had passed, but he could check on the party interface to see that Sunny was still alive somewhere and at max health. "Probably decided to do the light puzzle."

"Should we try to find him?"

"I mean, if you want, but if you die in a dungeon, you don't get any of the XP from it."

They sat in silence for a little longer.

Brackets clicked the end of one of his hooves on the stone floor as he felt himself get red again. Should he tell Valkyrie why he wanted to go to the dungeon?

Oh, what did it matter. Brackets had been too shy to tell Sunny who was then completely ruining their chances at doing what he wanted to.

Brackets was a glitch hunter, and there was no glitch more sought in the game than trying to unlock the NSFW content that seemed just barely inaccessible. Pretty much any mob that a glitch hunter had successfully clipped into seemed to have extra modeling inside of them in the crotch area, modeling always drawn but always hidden by clothes that couldn't be taken off or, in the naga's case, a vent that was unable to open.

Brackets was one of the top researchers in what mobs did and didn't appear to have the extra modeling, but no monster captured his attention more than the nagas. He'd tried with absolutely no avail to somehow trigger the sexual animations they had to have, despite the fact he was one of the most prolific glitch hunters in the forums. Had they removed all the underlying code for sex, but just never fixed the models? Or was there just something he hadn't tried?

Brackets could feel himself getting wet under the tunic. *Wet.* That wasn't a thing that was allowed to happen in the game before.

After checking that Valkyrie wasn't looking, he carefully slid a hand between his legs and up his tunic to discover that his underwear wasn't drawn and he was *wet* and *puffy*.

He bit his lower lip and tried to forget it.

"I think he's probably cleared enough mobs where I can solve the light puzzle for him," He eventually said.

He wriggled until he got his hooves under him and shakily rose to a stand. After equipping his crutches, he headed down the main hall with intent to solve the light puzzle he assumed Sunny was stuck on.

As he walked, the rubber tips of his crutches went *tpt* against the stone floor as his hooves gave a soft *clip*. The pattern *tpttpt clip,clip. tpttpt clip,clip* sounded down in echoes.

The main hall was empty down to the boss door. The dungeon was incredibly short if someone simply wanted to hoof through it even if it was mostly popular for its detailed side areas.

With planted hooves, Brackets wedged his shoulder against one of the double stone doors to the boss room and pushed with all his might. Slowly, it edged open.

The room was also empty, no Sunny to be found.

Maybe Sunny was somewhere searching for clues on how to solve the puzzle, clues that didn't exist. The light puzzle's starting configuration was randomized every time the dungeon was loaded in to prevent looking up the answer, and beyond that, it required a sort of rubik's cube logic to solve, something that couldn't just be written in a journal somewhere.

Brackets approached the upright sarcophagus in the middle of the room. He pressed one of the nine gems imbedded in it to watch the pattern change.

Pressing one caused every other gem to change whether it was on or off. The goal was to get every gem to glow at the same time. It wasn't a puzzle that Brackets was good at the first time he had come, but he had solved it so many times that he no longer understood why anyone else struggled with it.

As soon as he hit the last gem, he dispelled his crutches and used his nimble deer legs to leap backwards, just barely fast enough to miss the stone door falling forwards onto the ground with a massive thump.

Despite managing to avoid the first trap, vine-textured snakes burst out from the floor and wrapped around Brackets's legs.

The first spell the boss always cast was a de-mobilizing one, and the second action was attacking the nearest player. In his haste to solve the Incredibly Easy Light Puzzle, he'd forgotten that he was level one. He was usually 85 so he could survive long enough to try and invoke new animations.

The eyes of the boss opened from within the coffin, and a sharp-fanged grin stretched across his snake-like face. King Somber, as he was called, was tightly folded up to fit in the massive stone building and held a decorative polearm.

But he didn't go for the kill.

Brackets felt his heart begin to race as the vine-snake tongues flickered on his legs. He could swear they were slowly moving up, slowly following his wanting smell inside the tunic. It was too slow to be sure.

Somber turned his head down at Brackets and began to slither out. Where other nagas had the same torso size as humans, Somber's torso was the size of Brackets's entire body. He leaned down and lined his massive head vertical to Brackets's face, but he did not strike. No, he struck the polearm into the ground and used it as a leaning post before chuckling from his chest.

Brackets could feel the rumble in his own ribs. He had to be beet red. He had to be stupid.

"Thought I wouldn't recognize you?" the naga hummed in a laugh. He extended one index to lay his claw under Brackets's chin. "You adventures may change species, but you never do change face, and I've seen yours around much more than most." His scaly hand slid down Brackets's jaw until his thumb laid on the cheek and his webbed fingers wrapped about the back of the head.

Brackets tensed up, correctly reading the emotion in those dazzling green eyes but refusing to believe it.

"At least you've made a deeper impression than most."

The vine snakes tightened their coil on Brackets's leg. His wetness dripped, and he felt it get lapped up by a curious, leafy tongue.

"You would come here in armor I couldn't possibly beat, with strength I couldn't possibly escape, and yet you would more often than not immobilize me as I have done to you now, and then you'd try to break the barrier we've been trying to break for ages." Somber let his other hand under Brackets's long tunic and gripped Brackets's pussy. His slick pooled in the webbing of Somber's fingers.

Brackets remained too stunned to speak. He just looked over the massive naga and the gold jewelry that made its only clothes.

"And finally you break that barrier somehow, and then you come to me in this weakened, fragile state."

Somber tightened his grips on Brackets's neck and sex as the vine snakes multiplied and crawled further up. They slipped under the belt of the tunic and wrapped over his torso. They ran down his arms and forced them to cross behind him.

"Now, what does that say to me?"

"Says I think I can beat you without taking a hit," Brackets joked, but his sly smirk was quickly melted when the snakes lifted him slightly from the ground and split his legs.

Somber's finger re-adjusted and rubbed on Brackets's opening. "I think you under-estimate how long I've been dreaming of ravaging you," Somber growled through his dripping venom. "How hungry I am to lash years of sexual frustration into you."

Brackets hummed under the feel of the nagas thick finger pressing on its opening. The only reason it hadn't yet popped in was the fact it was incredibly thick. He compartmentalized that pleasure and looked Somber in the eye. He tried to pull his lips back into a cocked grin and huffed, "Right now it looks like you only know how to tease."

The naga leaned back as he let his massive tongue slither in and out of his mouth. The entangling snakes coiled tighter, further. One's snout pressed into Brackets's wetness, let its own small tongue into him.

Brackets groaned through clenched teeth as he wriggled in his binds. The tongue was too small to please, too quick to build tension, and yet its stimulation riled Brackets for what was to come, what he was still being denied.

"Tease, was it?"

Brackets couldn't respond as Somber moved his wet hand to Brackets's mouth. The pointed tip wedged his jaw open so that the scales slipped over his tongue, forcing him to taste his own slick.

"Didn't take long at all to wipe that smirk from your face, did it?" Somber pushed himself between Brackets's legs. The girth of his snake-like body squished between Brackets's thighs until they impeded progress, at which point the vines shifted to make Brackets more open.

The vent lined up with the pussy, wet heat on wet heat. The snake teasing Brackets retreated so that the hard corners of the vent could spread Brackets's lips as they opened.

Brackets moaned and shook in the vine-snakes, wanting desperately to take the soft bulge licking out against his opening. He was left unable to do so, both by his binds and his sex-induced stupidity.

"My, this really is such a small and fragile state for you." Somber, using the hand that didn't have a finger in Brackets's mouth, drew a claw harmlessly down Brackets's neck. "The moment I let you have even a little of me, that's going to be the end of you, isn't it?"

Brackets could only tense against the beast's scales.

"Take a deep breath, then," Somber hummed in a laugh. He grabbed Brackets's short blonde hair in his great hand. "Because I'm not letting up until I've had just as much fun."

A hot, dripping, soft appendage pressed through the vent and into Brackets. He fell limp in his binds as he reveled in the alien sensation of the pliable, tentacle-like dick worming perfectly into his body. It filled him passed his g-spot until it pressed the cervix as far as it would comfortably grow, and then it began to tense within him. The muscles grew thicker, firmer, and they writhed within Brackets.

Brackets stretched back against his binds and held his shoulders high as his body. The grip of ecstasy clawed up his back and dug into his skin.

When his orgasm came, it came *hard*. He moaned like a barbarian into the thumb still in his mouth and his body pulled at the vines holding him aloft and still.

But there was no break. No stopping. Somber leaned over Brackets so that his stomach laid across the faun's chest and face. Brackets could feel his antlers digging into Somber's skin, yet Somber didn't seem to notice or mind.

The added weight further reduced how Brackets could move. His hooves were as spread as they could be to make room for the oversized naga, and Somber had him completely pinned in the vine-snakes.

Still recovering, having had no time to catch his breath, Somber's appendage curled over itself to allow more length to push in. Brackets could do nothing, say nothing as he felt it ambitiously search his insides for space to grow.

Finally, the tip found it. It wiggled against the cervix and then squirmed. It softened as it had before to get in, but the rest of the tentacle stayed firm. The tip pushed and re-angled until finally, it slipped in. Soft, it homed in Brackets womb and curled and let another few inches of Somber in. A few inches more. With Brackets helpless, a foot. Two feet.

Each push, the tentacle sent waves of softness and firmness to let it worm further and then stake claim. Each push drove Brackets over the edge he had already careened over, and he moaned and drooled and writhed with a great continuous orgasm.

Somber ran out of length as the base was all the width Brackets's legs could afford. With that, the filling stopped, and Brackets finally found relief.

He breathed heavily under Somber and tried to collect his thoughts in the momentary break.

A moment was all Brackets got.

Somber took his hand from Brackets's mouth to wrap both arms around him as he tensed. His appendage, too, tensed and squirmed within.

Brackets gasped under the weight of the scales and relaxed for the massive member swirling around in him. His moans were finally audible, his pleasure feeding Somber's. He sunk in exhausted pleasure into the vines as they began to wilt and give with Somber's complete distraction. Slowly, Brackets was lowered into Somber's coiling tail, and then he was wrapped in muscular reptile.

The two orgasms had been all Brackets had in
him. Exhaustion and a hint of soreness set into his
little man-deer body. He relaxed and closed his eyes,
letting Somber spend the rest of himself in his
afterglow.

After some time, just enough for Brackets to quiet
down, he felt a new hot begin to fill him.

Cum. Lots of it. It filled his womb and dripped
out of him, and still it came. It ran down the white fur
of his legs and dripped into the coil. The tentacle lost
nearly all of his firmness inside.

Somber groaned as he loosened a bit against
Brackets.

"Done?" Brackets huffed between breaths.

"You came twice," Somber hissed. "I said I'm
staying until I've had the same amount of fun." He
turned Brackets around and bent him over the coil.
His dick re-hardened, somehow feeling even larger in
the new angle. "So long as you're not a dumb slut
that'll cum a third time, this should be quick."

It was not quick.

5: Valkyrie Finds an Iron Maiden, but With Less Spikes and More Tentacles

Valkyrie left pretty much as soon as Brackets did. She wasn't terribly worried about losing the experience given she didn't really care about leveling up, so she just walked right around.

Once in the chiseled hall, she looked around and admired the craftsmanship of the place. Everything had been carved out of the mountain, and a nice braiding pattern snaked down the mid of the wall. The top of the walls blended into the ceiling with the glimmering gems above, never losing that sort of outdoors look.

There were many doors. Lots of them. She decided to just go in the first that caught her eye.

Beyond the stone door was a spiral staircase down. Echoing from below, she could hear someone talking.

Talking?

Moaning.

Rhythmically, yes, a voice was taking sharp inhales between outlets.

Valkyrie quickly looked behind her before continuing down the stairs in curiosity.

The room at the end of the staircase was shockingly small, though its walls were made of large, crude wooden doors locked shut. She could hear movement behind all of them, the moans behind one. The doors had a series of holes in them, perfect for jabbing a spear through. Another door seemed to be open, capable of shutting the little space off from the stairs.

The navigable space was claustrophobic, barely thick enough for Valkyrie to fit in, but sat in it, surrounded by the holes and the multiple audible nagas in stabby range, was a shitty little wooden treasure chest.

Oh, thought Valkyrie, who had never played an adventure game before. *I bet there's good stuff in there.*

She walked into the tiny little space and crouched down. As soon as she touched the chest, it burst into ash and the door shut behind her. A stalagmite dropped from the roof to finish the hinge, locking the door shut.

Valkyrie stood back up and pushed on the door. It wouldn't budge.

Something cold and wet touched her back and licked up her spine.

She spun around to see that a free-roaming pink tentacle was waving curiously about the little space. It was thicker at the base, yet feathered down to a more reasonable size at the end. There was a little flare there, making the tip almost spade-shaped, though the flare seemed just as soft and malleable as the rest of the appendage.

The limb seemed particularly fond of her. it tried to bore into her warmth, though it only slid across her dark skin. It aimlessly drew scribbles of wetness on her stomach until it wandered up under her top and between her boobs. It continued up over her jawline and pressed on her lips.

Curious, she ran a hand down the shaft. It gave almost completely to her touch, able to condense down to much thinner than it really was.

She was *pretty* sure she was supposed to get fucked by that thing or something, but maybe it was like fall damage, just some sort of attack she was immune to. Either way, she decided to taste it.

As soon as she let out her tongue to taste its salt, the tip softened enough to sneak under her teeth and then thicken in her mouth.

Okay, this was definitely for fucking.

With a shrug, she closed her eyes and built just a little suction around it. She held the tentacle with one hand as she let her other work down to her dick. Her thumb gently woke it as the tentacle sent a wave of softness out. With it, it dove deeper into her mouth, and then it hardened and pulled her forward.

She yelped with shock, though it was completely muffled, but then relaxed. It was calling her forward.

Another wave of softness, and it dove into her throat. She moved herself closer to the hole. Two more tugs, and she was on her knees, her mouth against the hole. Still, the tentacle drew into her.

As she aroused her dick to full length, she felt something touch it. She had to crane a bit to look down enough to see scaly fingers reaching for her from another lower hole.

Well, she was polite, so she scooted forward. As she stuck herself in, she felt it enter what she could only guess was monster pussy. It was wet and warm, but quite open for interpretation.

Her dick slid in with complete ease until it brushed a firm organ somewhere inside. Like a snare trap, the entryway clenched around her, trapping her lovely, firm, pillowy hotness.

With a pleasured moan, she softly thrust and sucked, though she had a feeling that the nagas didn't move much during sex. The tentacle continued to send waves of firmness and the vagina did the same, as if sucking on her, as if pushing something into her endlessly.

She could hear scratching in the walls. Moans and talking.

More tentacles worked out of the remaining holes and made for her. They wrapped around her body and coated her in their sweet slime. They worked between her braids and harmlessly coiled over her neck.

Filled and bound, Valkyrie relaxed into the squirming embrace of wet and hungry strangers. They curiously wormed about her body, over her chest and thighs and any exposed skin. One slipped its tip down the dip of her spine, between her soft muscles, and then between her ass cheeks. It let itself into her with its waves of firmness, and she could only moan in pleasure.

Calm in the mass of tentacles, she let the pleasures of her dick and g-spot build in her stomach. She held tight to the wall, and she let her tension slip down. Like sitting down after a long day, like smiling at a lover after waking from a dream, the ills of her body spirited away as she came.

She stayed still for a few moments as she collected her post-nut thoughts. She wasn't the type to keep an extra in the chamber, an ejaculate-and-evacuate kind of girl, so it only took a few moments before she leaned back and out of the tentacle in her mouth. Her soft dick slipped from its own space. She realized how tired she was, so she sat with her back leaned against the back door as she watched the tentacles start to find each other.

With a splintering rip, the door seemed to vanish from behind her, and she toppled onto her back. Looking up, she first saw Sunny's dick and then his sharp-toothed grin.

"I see you're having fun in the trap room," he laughed.

She gave him a thumbs up.

"So is Brackets. He's probably going to be a while, so I packed us a lunch," he said, materializing a massive roast from his inventory.

"Ooo." Valkyrie rolled to her stomach, tried to brush some of the slime off, and walked as they talked about their adventures.

6: It's About the Lore. The Lore!

Once in an inn, Sunny pulled up his menu. "Hm. Still can't leave. Guess that patch really messed something up."

"Man, I didn't even get to level up," Brackets muttered as he collapsed on the bed. Though his words spoke annoyance, his tone was blissed out.

"Yeah, how'd you manage to die on your way back?" Valkyrie snickered.

"There's this drop off before a good piece of loot, and I'm really used to the potion glitch working." He blew a raspberry.

"Eh, you wouldn't have made it to level three anyway," Sunny said. "The only thing that got us experience was you solving that light puzzle."

"Well, you didn't kill anything."

"It felt sort of rude to."

"Yeah, hey, Valkyrie, since you got all the experience with Sunny maxed and me having died, shouldn't you be level two?"

Valkyrie blinked and opened her menu to inspect herself, but when she did, she saw a big shiny LEVEL

UP button at the top. "Oh, I guess this is it." She clicked it, and she felt wings burst from her back. The x-shape of the robes that made her top perfectly avoided where they came from her, and dark feathers puffed out and slowly sank around the room. She looked at them and grabbed them, massive gray appendages that felt nearly weightless to her.

"Whoa. Does this mean I can fly?"

"Not really, you have to be pretty high level for actual flight, but you can stop yourself midair, now," Sunny said.

Valkyrie immediately jumped and spread her wings. She stayed there, levitating off the ground. She gave the two fellas a very excited grin before accidently dispelling the wings and falling on her ass.

"You know, I knew it," Brackets said without provocation. "I *knew* this game had sex animations and fully detailed mobs, but I couldn't prove it. I mean, that was *not* human genitalia. The writers made an entirely new reproductive system, but all that lore just got thrown out when they decided this 18+ game had to be child friendly."

"Financial companies." Sunny shook his head.

"Hey. While we're here, why don't we try to figure out as much of this lore as we can before they reinstate the adult content filter? Make forums, you know."

Sunny stroked his scaly chin. "Yeah. Plus, what if there's some other players here that haven't figured out that sex got set to yes? I'd feel pretty bad if I missed out on this."

Valkyrie searched through all the drawers until she found some parchment and ink. "Yeah! Let's compile what we learned or whatever."

And so the three talked for a while in their room and wrote until they perfected a forum. They all traveled downstairs and pinned it to the inn's corkboard before reading over it.

The Nagas of Night's Edge Dungeon

The nagas, despite almost no sexual dimorphism, have two distinct sexes similar to human sexes.

The males have tentacle dicks that are malleable and several feet long. This is to accommodate for the unusually long and curled vaginal canal of the females. The dicks are self-lubricating and soften/harden in waves to encourage working through the long canal. Likewise, the females have a small organ near their entrance that, when stimulated, cause them to clench down on whatever is inside of them. Their flesh also has this wave pattern to draw the dick in.

They don't move or thrust much during sex like we do, instead relying on their internal movement to do the work for them.

Sunny: Don't be intimidated by the size of the males if you're trying to stick your dick in. Their vaginas are pretty good at changing to your shape! However, I'm not the biggest fan of how they don't move much. I like action, myself.

Brackets: The boss is also fuckable, but you are going to have to solve that light puzzle to get to him. If you do, he will absolutely trap you and have his way with you. I recommend, but only if you're into the idea of having five foot of wriggling, muscular tentacle in you. Maybe pack a stamina potion?

Valkyrie: spear room full of dicks 10/10

Bonus

"Hey," Sunny realized. "You just need to be able to set a campfire, right? To test your glitch?"

Brackets nodded.

"Why don't I put down the campfire for you?"

"That'd work, but I just didn't want to bother someone about it."

Sunny materialized lumber. "I've got you. Get ready."

Brackets readied his polearm and focused on the lumber. When Sunny threw it down, Brackets stabbed forward and struck the blade between the campfire and ground. The lumber split, but then changed model to the campfire base. It stuck to the ground below and bellowed the fire effect.

Brackets did not go flying back as he had hoped. Instead, his spear held stuck between the campfire and the ground no matter how much he tugged it, so he eventually just unequipped it.

"Guess that's bust," Sunny muttered.

"Well, I have confirmed that it doesn't become part of the map like I had thought and is a separate entity stuck to it, but it could still cause physics issues. I'd have to try at least a hundred more times to make sure this isn't a viable thing."

"You know, now I see why you wanted to do it yourself."

About the Author

I used to play World of Warcraft a lot (too much, some may say). The game has changed a lot since I played it, but it used to have a very important boat system. If you wanted to get to another continent, you had to take a boat, and even if you were going to the same continent, it was often faster to take a boat than it was to fly.

If you were in the alliance, this meant you had to use Stormwind Harbor a *lot*. Not only did it have the most active boat lines, but the city of Stormwind had everything in it. However, Stormwind is significantly above sea-level, so when you went to the harbor, there was this big drop-off. There were ramps down, but they were sort of out of the way and the boats were *right in front of you.*

Naturally, this meant everyone jumped down the cliff.

However, unlike most other games, distance fallen was calculated as a flat number instead of a percentage of your total health. This meant that there were falls you'd survive at a higher level that would have killed you at a lower.

If you were human, you'd probably reach Stormwind harbor for the first time around level 10. Other alliance races reached it around 15. I'm not sure at what level you started surviving that fall, but it was greater than 15.

This meant that the first time you go to Stormwind Harbor, you'd see this cliff and the boats just out of your reach, and you think, *oh, that's too far of a fall. I have to take the ramp.* Right after you think that, you see some level 45 bozo launch himself right off the wall. He takes some damage, sure, but he'll heal up on the boat ride. So, you decide to jump yourself.

And you die.

(I'm going to be very embarrassed if I'm misremembering this)

www.ingramcontent.com/pod-product-compliance
Lightning Source LLC
Chambersburg PA
CBHW020939160726
47993CB00007B/2840